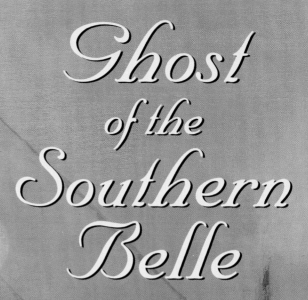

Ghost
of the
Southern
Belle

A SEA TALE

by **Odds Bodkin**

Paintings by
Bernie Fuchs

Little, Brown and Company
Boston   New York   London

It was from the deck of my father's schooner that I first saw Captain LeNoir leave his wheel and dance across the deck of the *Southern Belle*.

"Did you see that, Father?" I cried, amazed. Even with no one at her helm, LeNoir's *Southern Belle* raced past us, leaving a merry fiddler's tune in her wake. Full of codfish, our schooner *Candace* was slow and heavy in the swells.

"The man's mad," grumbled Father. "Thinks he's protected from the dangers of the sea."

That night we took a berth next to the *Southern Belle* in Gloucester Harbor. As I rinsed our deck, I came upon Captain LeNoir seated on his gunwale, tapping his boot heel. I'd heard that the Confederate captain had sailed north from New Orleans just to race Yankees.

"Why do you race our boats?" I demanded. "You know you're faster than any ship in our fleet."

"Ah, my little *capitaine,*" he said, smiling, "perhaps I long to be beaten, just once." Then something near him chimed faintly, like faraway bells.

"What's making that sound?" I asked.

LeNoir opened his palm to reveal two silver spheres, inlaid with Chinese symbols. "My protection," he whispered. "This one's Luck. This one's Daring." He tossed a sphere at me. I couldn't believe I caught it.

"Pure luck!" He laughed. "Keep it, then, my little *capitaine.*" His voice faded away as he dipped below deck.

From that night on, I never went on deck without the silver sphere. If a ship captain says something brings him luck, I believe him, even if he is a Rebel. The Chinese ball chimed merrily as I ran surefooted across the decks, bringing bait boards to Father's crew. I kept the token a secret. Father would have scoffed at my superstition.

On All Hallows' Eve, a nor'easter began to blow. At least fifty schooners were anchored with us on Georges Bank. Suddenly the *Molly Pitcher*'s anchor line snapped. The deadly storm drove her toward the *Southern Belle* and our *Candace.* To avoid a collision, we axed our anchor lines and sailed for harbor. LeNoir was soon ahead of us.

Father called out from the wheel, "The man's insane! He's sailing too close to shore. He'll never clear the point!"

In horror we watched as the *Southern Belle* slammed into the rocks. The screech of splintering boards and ripping cloth paralyzed me. Her mast toppled. As she listed to port, her crew scrambled to the high side. Waves crashed onto her decks, washing men into the sea.

"We've got to rescue them!" I yelled over the wind.

"We don't dare, son!" cried Father, desperately spinning his wheel as a blast of wind hit our sails. "Not in this storm! I won't risk this ship. Or you!"

I stumbled below. It is an unspoken law of the sea that if a crew is in danger, the nearest vessel must try to help. But we hadn't even lowered a dory! I took the Chinese sphere out of my pocket, wondering if I could be the reason that Captain LeNoir's luck had run out. Had he really given it to me?

All at once the shining orb fogged over. It turned as cold as the icy sea. Droplets trickled down its sides into my palm. I tasted one — it was salt water! As I slumped against a bulk-head, a terrible feeling swept over me. I shoved the sphere deep into my pocket and didn't dare touch it for the rest of the trip.

We made it safely to harbor. Grateful to be on dry land, I
ran to the beach the next morning. Usually flotsam washed
ashore from a wreck. Masts. Tackle. Barrels. Planking.
Wave after wave pounded ashore, but strangely the beach
was clear. How could there be no trace of the *Southern Belle*?

A series of deadly sinkings soon followed. Sailors watched gathering storm clouds with dread. Which ship's anchor line would mysteriously snap next, forcing her to race for her life? In the streets of Gloucester, some sailors blamed the wrecks on the harsh storms, but others whispered of a ghost ship. After the lighthouse keeper reported sighting a pale vessel racing alongside a doomed schooner just before she sank, all of Gloucester knew the seas were haunted.

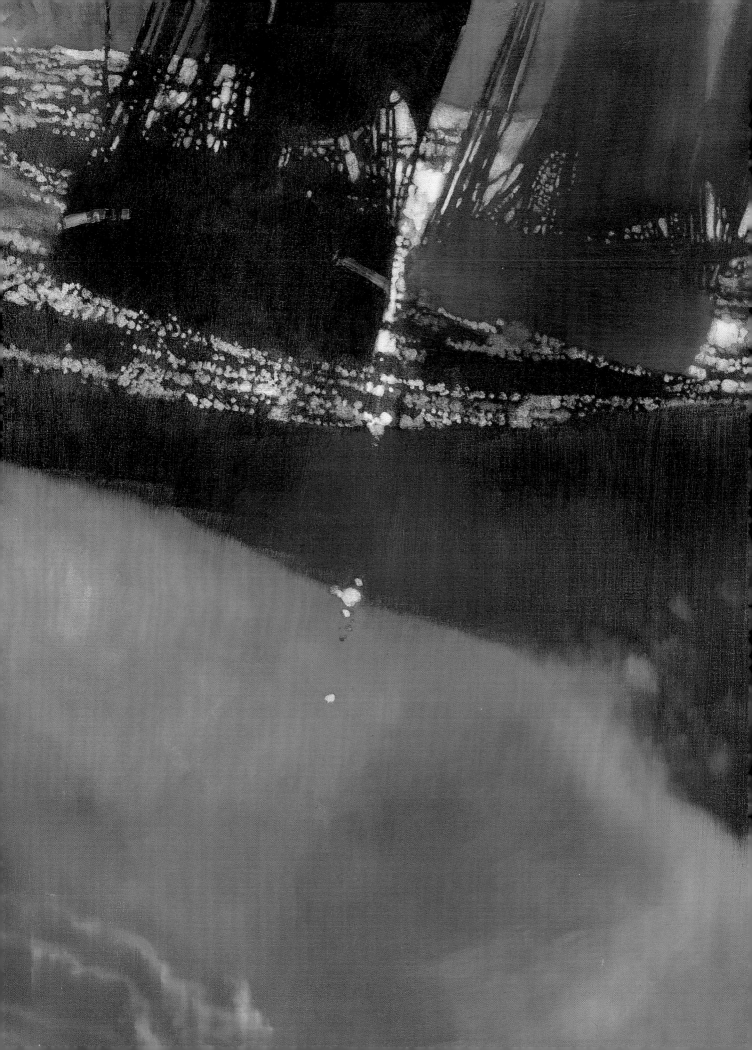

My silver sphere dripped salt water whenever the *Southern Belle* chased down her next opponent. LeNoir's ghost was angry, I knew. No one had tried to rescue his crew. Now the *Southern Belle* wasn't racing our sailors for sport. She was racing them for their lives. But Father was so scornful of superstitions, how could I convince him of the truth?

In late November, my chance came. Two schooners, in dire straits, appeared off the point. One was the *Faery Queen,* a ship we knew. She was racing beam to beam with an unknown schooner. Ashore for supplies, Father and I ran to the beach.

As the other schooner passed her bow, the *Faery Queen* keeled over and sank for no reason we could see. Her opponent heaved into a spume cloud and disappeared. We waited to spy her again. But we didn't. She was gone.

I handed my Chinese ball to my father. It was cold and dripping. I explained how I got it. "It's the *Southern Belle,* Father," I said quietly. "It's LeNoir, taking all our ships."

Father gazed out over the thundering breakers.

"I think I know how to stop him," I said.

Father listened to my plan. Just before we next set sail for Georges Bank, he called the crew together. "Gentlemen," Father said, "too many good men have been lost to what I'm now convinced is a ghost ship. Something has to be done for the safety of the fleet. My son has a plan to rid the seas of this curse. With luck, it will work."

I held up the gleaming ball for the crew to see as they listened to my plan. Some shook their heads and left. But most stayed.

The next week, we anchored on Georges Bank. But we didn't fish. We waited for a storm. Finally, on New Year's Eve, storm clouds gathered on the horizon and the breeze started to stir. Father and I stood at the helm with our eyes glued to the shining silver ball.

Hours later, as winds howled through the shrouds, the silver dulled. Moisture beaded on the sphere's curves. It was time to test my luck.

With Father by my side, I took the helm, and he ordered that the sails be hoisted. The eerie glow of the *Southern Belle* was off our stern; she was headed in our direction.

"Tonight LeNoir races us!" I yelled out to the crew, trying to sound like my father. Our boat was light and speedy. All through the stormy night, *Candace* held her lead as the *Southern Belle* chased us.

As dawn lit the churning, rain-swept sea, LeNoir was upon us. With my father navigating, I steered close to the point. Trying to steal our wind, LeNoir suddenly sprinted between our *Candace* and the submerged rocks. Our masts nearly collided.

"She's drawn abeam, Cap'n!" yelled Frye, the first mate, with terror in his voice.

I looked upwind at the ghost of the mad LeNoir and thrust my silver sphere into the air.

"Do you want it back?" I cried. When he saw who I was, he jumped across his deck to the gunwale. Behind him, the wheel spun madly out of control, rounding his ship up into the wind. "Your luck is still mine!" I yelled.

LeNoir's unearthly eyes fixed upon me. I stared back, counting the seconds. Suddenly his ship shuddered and slammed into the rocks just as it had the year before.

Our crewmen cheered as we sped away. But I knew the threat of the ghost ship was still alive.

"Prepare to come about!" I ordered.

"But we can round the point!" cried the first mate.

"No! Break out the dory! Prepare for a rescue!" I commanded. Father nodded. He understood.

As *Candace* made her wide turn to tack back into the wind, we could see the *Southern Belle* heeled over and awash, crewmen clinging to her masts. Captain LeNoir gripped his wheel on the tilted deck.

"Sail her in close, mate," Father ordered, jumping down into the dory, "then on into harbor without fail! We must rescue these men." I jumped in with him.

"But Cap'n," Frye protested, "they're ghosts!"

"Lower away. Time is short!" *Candace* slid away as our dory splashed through the icy water.

With all our strength, we rowed toward the sinking ship.

"Captain LeNoir!" I hollered, cupping my hands. "Prepare to be rescued!"

But already the salt spray was whisking through him. "You need not put us in your boat, my little *capitaine,*" he called over the wind, "to have rescued us at last!" His mainmast crashed to the deck. Ignoring it, he tossed something to me. It was the other Chinese ball! As I caught it, it chimed merrily, warm and polished.

"You already have Luck!" he called. "That one's for Daring! *Merci,* brave Yankee. At last we are free!"

Then Captain LeNoir and his men looked up into the howling storm and cheered. And for the last time — this time forever — the *Southern Belle* vanished into the spume.

For Jonathan, Gavin, and Christopher
— O. B.

For Babe
— B. F.

Text copyright ©1999 by Rivertree Productions, Inc.
Illustrations copyright © 1999 by Bernie Fuchs

First Edition

Library of Congress Cataloging-in-Publication Data

Bodkin, Odds.
    Ghost of the Southern Belle : a sea tale / by Odds Bodkin ; paintings by Bernie
Fuchs. — 1st ed.
        p.   cm.
    Summary: The young son of a ship's captain finds a way to end the curse of
a ghost ship whose daring Confederate captain once gave him a lucky ball.
    ISBN 0-316-02608-5
    [1. Shipwrecks — Fiction. 2. Ghosts — Fiction.] I. Fuchs, Bernie, ill. II. Title.
PZ7.B6355Gh 1999
[Fic] — dc21   98-15778

10 9 8 7 6 5 4 3 2 1

SC

Printed in Hong Kong

The paintings for this book were done in oil on canvas.
The text was set in Calisto, and the display type is Nuptial Script.